Your Grumpy Green

by Liza Charlesworth

ISBN: 978-1-338-78279-0
Illustrated by Kevin Zimmer
Copyright © 2021 by Liza Charlesworth. All rights reserved.
Published by Scholastic Inc., 557 Broadway, New York, NY 10012

10 9 8 7 6 5 4 3 2 1   68   21 22 23 24 25 26 27/0

Printed in Jiaxing, China. First printing, June 2021.

Your green frog is grumpy.
He does not like pants.

2

Your green frog is grumpy.
He does not like plants.

Your green frog is grumpy.
He does not like hats.

4

Your green frog is grumpy.
He does not like cats.

Your green frog is grumpy.
He does not like stew.

Hop, hop, hop!

7

Your green frog is grumpy.
But he DOES like you!